Weekly Reader Books presents

Hester
the Jester

by Ben Shecter

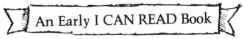

An Early I CAN READ Book

Harper & Row, Publishers

New York, Hagerstown, San Francisco, London

This book is a presentation of Weekly Reader Books.
Weekly Reader Books offers book clubs for children from
preschool through high school.

For further information write to:
Weekly Reader Books
4343 Equity Drive
Columbus, Ohio 43228

Library of Congress Cataloging in Publication Data
Shecter, Ben.
    Hester the jester

    (An Early I can read book)
    SUMMARY: A small girl wants to be something
important, but can't decide whether to be a jester, a
knight, or a king.
    I.   Title.
PZ7.S5382He3   [E]   76-58706
ISBN 0-06-025599-4
ISBN 0-06-025600-1 lib. bdg.

I Can Read Book is a registered trademark of Harper & Row,
Publishers, Inc.

For Emily

Chapter 1

Hester's father was a jester.

He danced.

He sang.

He told riddles.

He made funny faces.

Hester said,

"I want to be a jester!"

Her mother said, "No!"

Her father said, "No! No!"

Hester said, "Yes, yes, yes!"

In her room

Hester danced,

sang,

told riddles,

and made funny faces.

7

Hester's mother

caught her doing this.

She said,

"Stop the dances,

the songs,

the riddles,

and the funny faces."

Hester said, "Why?"

Her mother said,

"Girls cannot be jesters!"

8

"But I want to be a jester
like father," said Hester.

Chapter 2

The king was sad.

He called for the jester.

"Jester, make me laugh!"

said the king.

The jester danced, sang,

told riddles,

and made funny faces.

The king did not laugh.

"Go away," he said.

"I am still sad."

The jester's wife asked,

"Why are you sad?"

"I could not make the king laugh,"

said the jester.

When Hester saw her father sad,

she said, "I'll make you laugh!"

She danced and sang.

She told riddles.

She made funny faces.

Hester's father laughed.

"I will take you to the king,"

he said. "You will make him laugh."

"A girl jester?"

asked her mother.

"Why not!" said her father.

"Why not!" said Hester.

"Why not?" said her mother.

15

Chapter 3

The king was still sad.

"My little girl will make you laugh," said the jester.

"A girl jester?" asked the king.

"Why not!" said the jester.

"Why not!" said Hester.

"Why not?" said the king.

Hester danced,

sang,

told riddles,

and made funny faces.

The king laughed.

Hester laughed too.

"I feel silly," said Hester.

"Why?" asked the king.

"I feel silly making you laugh,"
she said. "I don't want
to be a jester anymore."

"What do you want to be?"
asked the king.

"I want to be something important,"
said Hester.

"Important?" asked the king.

"Important!" said Hester.

"I want to be a knight!"

"A knight?" asked the king.

"A knight!" said Hester.

The king made Hester a knight.

He gave her a horse.

He gave her a banner.

He gave her a sword.

She rode the horse.

She waved the banner.

She asked,

"What shall I do with the sword?"

"The sword is for battle!"

said the king.

"I don't want to battle," said Hester.

"Knights battle," said the king.

21

"I don't want to battle,"

said Hester. "I don't want

to be a knight anymore."

"What do you want to be?"

"Something more important!"

said Hester.

"More important?" asked the king.

"I want to be a king," said Hester.

"A king?" asked the king.

"A king!" said Hester.

"You're a king!" said the king.

"What does a king do?"

asked Hester.

"You listen to the people,"

said the king,

"and give advice."

"I will listen!" said Hester.

"And give advice."

They came

from near and far.

A farmer.

A milkman.

A hunter.

A mother.

The farmer said,

"My cat is away,

the rats are in the hay."

"Let the rats stay," said Hester.

"Silly advice!"

said the farmer.

The milkman said,

"My cows run dry,

my children cry."

"Let them eat apple pie,"

said Hester.

"Silly advice," said the milkman.

The hunter said,

"My dog is sick,

he can't run quick."

"Get a hunting cat instead,"

said Hester.

"Silly advice," said the hunter.

The mother said,

"My little girl has become a king,

have you ever heard of such a thing!"

The mother was sad.

Hester danced,

sang,

told riddles,

and made funny faces.

She made her mother laugh.

"I want to be your little girl again,"
said Hester.

"Good!" said her mother.

"Good!" said her father.

"Very good!" said the king.